PePPa Goes to HOLLYWOOD

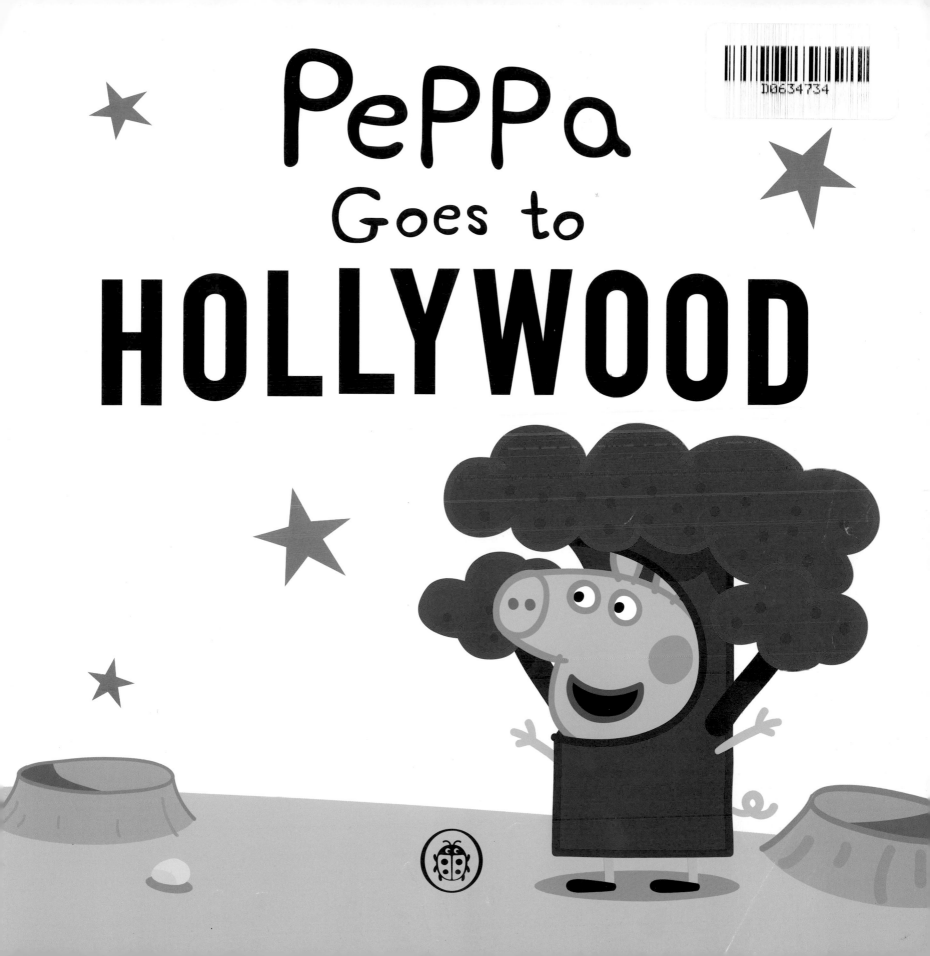

Peppa and George were watching their favourite superhero, Super Potato, on television.

"Win a trip to America to star in my new film, *Vegetables in Space*!" announced Super Potato. "Just find my Golden Ticket to join me and my co-star, Hash Brown, here in Hollywood!"

"Ooooh!" gasped Peppa.

Peppa ran into the kitchen where Mummy and Daddy Pig
were making dinner.
"Mummy," said Peppa, "can we find Super Potato's
Golden Ticket, *pleeease*?"
"There's only one ticket in the whole world, Peppa,"
said Mummy Pig. "We'd have to be *very* lucky to find it."

Just then, Mummy Pig said, "Oh! There's something in this potato!"
"It's the Golden Ticket!" gasped Peppa and Daddy Pig.
"We're going to **America!**" cried Mummy Pig.

A few days later, they were on the plane.
"This is your captain speaking," announced their pilot,
Miss Rabbit. "We'll soon be arriving in America . . . I think.
Does anyone know where it is?"
"Is that it?" asked Peppa, peering through the window.

Peppa was right . . . it *was* America!

Outside the airport, a bright-yellow taxi arrived to collect them.

The driver looked very familiar. "Miss Rabbit at your service!

Where d'ya wanna go?"

"You're Miss Rabbit?" gasped Peppa. "We have
a Miss Rabbit at home!"

"Every town needs a Miss Rabbit!" said the taxi driver. "Hop in!"

"Is this Hollywood?" asked Mummy Pig.
"No," said Miss Rabbit. "This is New York – the
city that never sleeps! I'll give you a tour."
New York was **very** busy – and **very** big.

Beep!

TAXI

POLICE

Beep!

Miss Rabbit got Peppa and George ice creams, then
took everyone to the first stop on her New York tour ...
the Empire State Building!
When they reached the top, Daddy Pig closed his eyes.
"I can't look," he said.

"But there's so much to see, Daddy!" cried Peppa. Miss Rabbit popped on her tour-guide cap. "With this telescope, you can see the Statue of Liberty!" she said.

Peppa looked through the telescope and across New York Harbor.

Hee!

Hee!

"I can see a big green lady with an ice cream!" she cried, holding her own cone in the air. "Look at me! I'm the Statue of Liberty!"

The next stop was Times Square. "Look!" called Peppa, pointing at a billboard. "That's the film we're going to be in!" "You need to go to Hollywood!" said Miss Rabbit. "I have just the thing to get you there . . ."

"... a motorhome!" said Miss Rabbit. She threw Daddy Pig the keys, and Peppa's family climbed aboard.

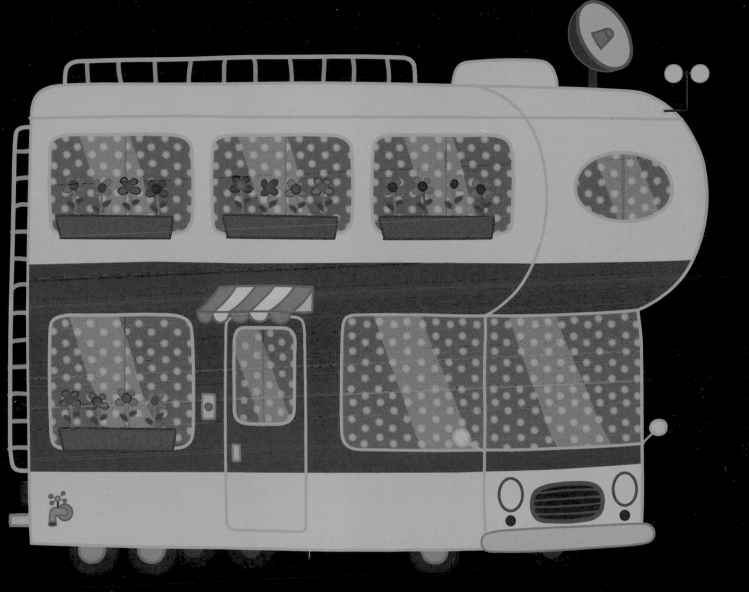

It had been a very busy day in New York. Peppa
and her family needed a good night's rest in the
motorhome before the journey to Hollywood.
"For a city that never sleeps, it's made me
very sleepy," said Daddy Pig.

The next day, Peppa and her family got
straight on the road to Hollywood.
"Are we there yet, Daddy Pig?" asked Mummy Pig.
"Erm, let's ask someone," he replied.

Beep!

Beep!

They pulled up outside a nearby diner where someone
familiar-looking was strumming a guitar . . .
"Howdy, folks! I'm Miss Rabbit!"
"It's *another* Miss Rabbit!" Peppa cried.
"Yep! There are a lot of us around," replied Miss Rabbit. "Now,
what can I do for you? Do you need gas? Or a bite to eat?"

"Are we in Hollywood?" asked Mummy Pig.

"No, ma'am. You're a *looong* way from Hollywood!" said
Miss Rabbit. "But, as you're here, why don't you get some
home-cooking in your bellies?"

"Well, I suppose we *could* stop for breakfast," said Daddy Pig.

After a delicious breakfast of eggs, Miss Rabbit took Peppa's family country dancing . . .

. . . and monster trucking! "Daddy's truck is jumping up and down in muddy puddles!" Peppa cheered.

But there was no time to waste if they were going to make it to the film set. Peppa and her family had to say goodbye.

"Hash Brown is my favourite actor," said Miss Rabbit. "Tell him 'howdy' from me!"

Daddy Pig drove for miles
and miles, until . . .
"STOP!" yelled Mr Bison.
"Canyon ahead! And if you
want to know more, there's an
information desk over there."

Peppa and her family met another Miss Rabbit at the information desk. She gave them a tour of the Grand Canyon in her helicopter. "Wow!" cried Peppa.

"Amazing, isn't it?" said Miss Rabbit. "These rocks have been here since the time of the dinosaurs!"
"Dine-saw! *Grrr!*" shouted George.

Miss Rabbit's tour continued with a ride down some rapids . . .

. . . and a visit to the Grand Canyon Caverns, where
she showed them animal pictures drawn a long time ago.
"Oooh!" cried George.

Daddy Pig drove out of the desert.
"Are we nearly there yet?" asked Peppa.
"I don't know," said Daddy Pig. "Let's stop
and look at the map!"

"Sir, did you know you must only stop on a freeway if it is an emergency?" said a police rabbit.

"It's *another* Miss Rabbit!" said Peppa. "Miss Rabbit, it *is* an emergency!"

"We've won tickets to be in Super Potato's new film, *Vegetables in Space*!" added Mummy Pig.

Nee-naa!

"In that case, head straight on until you see the Hollywood sign. If you don't see the sign, look out for the stars!" said Miss Rabbit. George spotted them first. "Star! Star!" he shouted. Then Peppa spotted two real-life stars. "It's Super Potato and Hash Brown!" she cried.

"We won the competition to be in your film,
Vegetables in Space!" said Peppa.
"Then let's get to the studio!" cried Super Potato.
"We've got a film to make!"

On the film set, Peppa and her family were
dressed up as broccoli, then the filming began . . .
"LIGHTS! CAMERA! ACTION!"
Hundreds of space-carrots zoomed towards
Super Potato and Hash Brown's spaceship.
"Oh no!" shouted Super Potato.
"These naughty carrots will
destroy the universe!"

"If only there were some way of getting rid of them!" cried Hash Brown.
"We could eat them," said Peppa. "But it looks like there are too many."

Clang!

Plink!

Clang!

Just then, some unexpected visitors arrived at the studio . . .
"Hello!" said several familiar voices. "We couldn't miss meeting Hash Brown!"
It was Miss Rabbit, Miss Rabbit, Miss Rabbit, Miss Rabbit and Miss Rabbit.

"We have to eat the carrots!" explained Peppa.
"It's to save the universe!"
The Miss Rabbits were very happy to help – they
loved carrots even more than they loved Hash Brown!

"We did it!" cried Super Potato.
"Hooray!" everyone cheered.
The universe was saved, thanks to Peppa and all the Miss Rabbits.
"Have you had a good time on your trip, Peppa?"
asked one Miss Rabbit.
"Yes!" said Peppa. "The best bit was ... everything!"

Peppa loves Hollywood.
Everyone loves Hollywood!